Our thanks to Janet Glass for the wonderful title.

enchantedlionbooks.com

First published in 2016 by Enchanted Lion Books,
351 Van Brunt Street, Brooklyn, NY 11231
Copyright © 2016 by Jorge Lujan for the text
Copyright © 2016 by Mandana Sadat for the illustrations
Copyright © 2016 by John Oliver Simon for
the English-language text
All rights reserved under International and Pan-American
Copyright Conventions
A CIP record is on file with the Library of Congress
ISBN 978-1-59270-194-0
Printed in China
10 9 8 7 6 5 4 3 2 1

Jorge Luján * Mandana Sadat

Translated from the Spanish by John Oliver Simon

Trunk
to
Trunklet

ENCHANTED LION BOOKS
NEW YORK

Mommy seal nuzzles
nose to nose with her pup.
Warm fur and whiskers
keep them snuggled up.

Bear cub sleeps so cozily
up on Mommy's shoulder.
He'll play with his sisters
when he's a little older!

Seeing myself in your eyes
how very small I get.
Now I know why you call me,
little owlet.

The tiger kitten is roaring
but his mom won't get upset.
She knows his baby fangs
can't bite anything yet.

Mommy's dancing branch to branch
high above a wall.
Her baby monkeys shield her eyes
for fear that she might fall.

Mommy's fur is an ocean wave
that she keeps silky and lush.
Her tongue cleans her kittens
like a watercolor brush.

Who's got a pocket
without any pants
to take her joeys walking
from Australia to France?

Mommy jabiru brings her chick
some food to swallow, *please*!
But the little one's distracted
by the tickling of fleas.

Little lambs wear sweaters
to guard against wind and storm.
Mommy is proud she knitted them
to keep her lambkins warm.

Cucu rucu cuuu,
mommy pigeon cries.
Rucu cucu ruuu,
baby pigeon tries.

At twilight on the prairie,
hear mommy elephant trumpet!
Her calf comes trotting back to her
and they play trunk to trunklet.

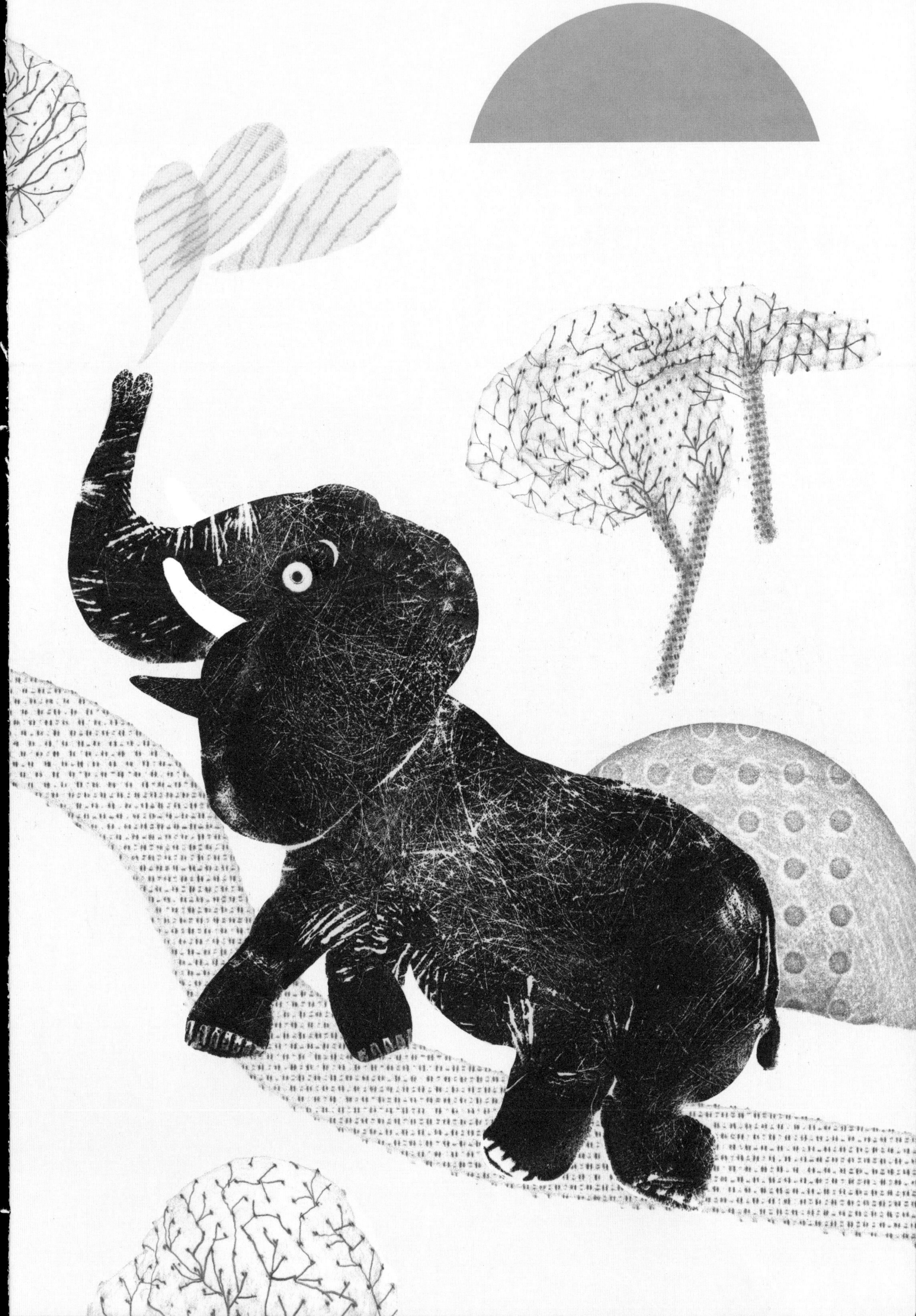

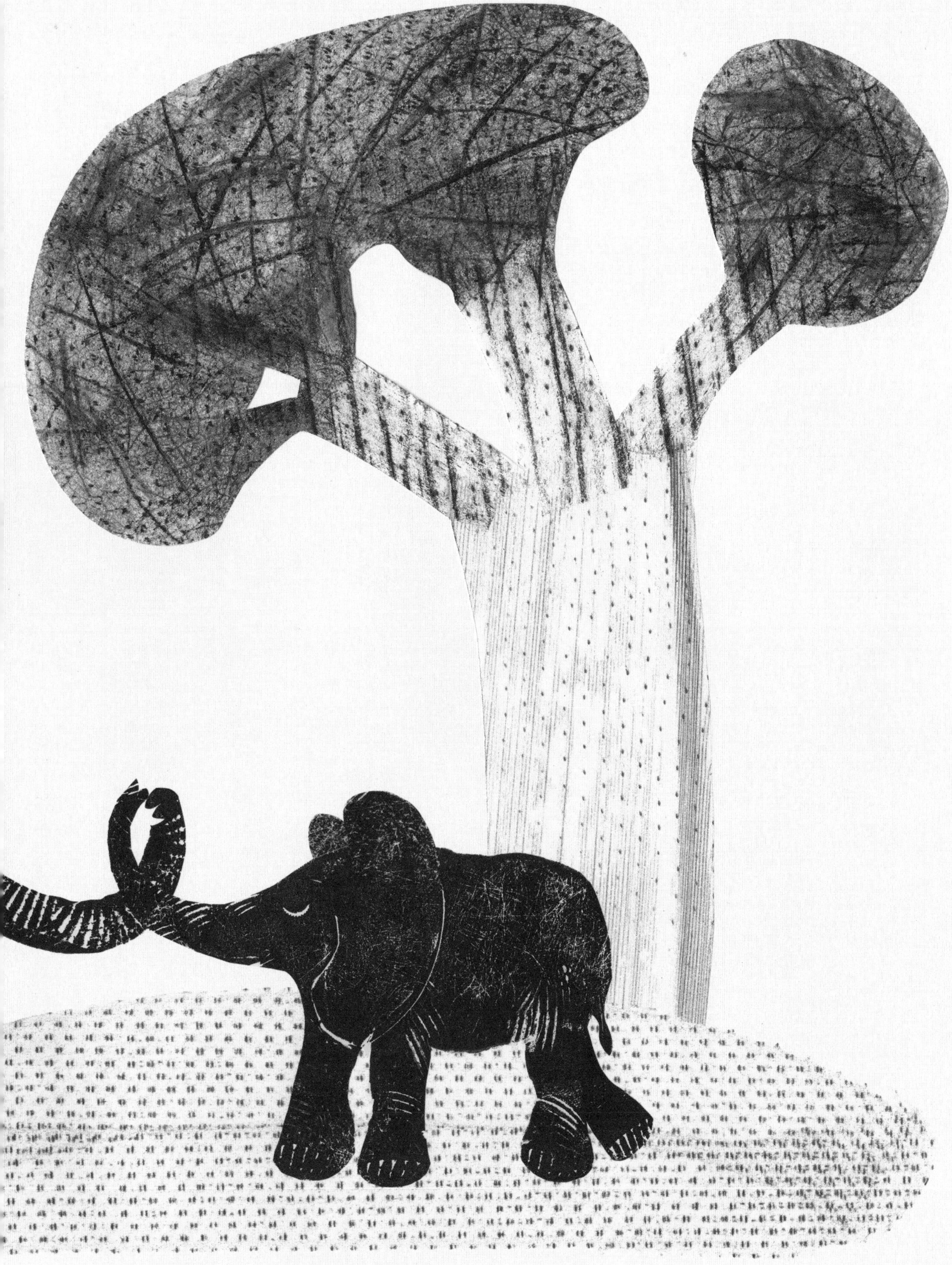